E BOIGER A
Boiger, Alexandra, author,
illustrator.
Max and Marla are flying
together

MAX AND MARLA

ARE FLYING TOGETHER

Fountaindale Public Library
Bolingbrook, IL
(630) 759-2102

ALEXANDRA BOIGER

PHILOMEL BOOKS

To my brother Fritz and my sister Angela, with love.

PHILOMEL BOOKS
an imprint of Penguin Random House LLC, New York

Copyright © 2019 by Alexandra Boiger.

Penguin supports copyright. Copyright fuels creativity, encourages diverse voices, promotes free speech, and creates a vibrant culture. Thank you for buying an authorized edition of this book and for complying with copyright laws by not reproducing, scanning, or distributing any part of it in any form without permission. You are supporting writers and allowing Penguin to continue to publish books for every reader.

Philomel Books is a registered trademark of Penguin Random House LLC.
Visit us online at penguinrandomhouse.com

Library of Congress Cataloging-in-Publication Data

Names: Boiger, Alexandra, author, illustrator.
Title: Max and Marla are flying together / Alexandra Boiger.
Description: New York : Philomel Books, [2019] | Summary: Max discovers that his best friend Marla, a snowy owl, is afraid to fly, and patiently encourages her to try.
Identifiers: LCCN 2018049757| ISBN 9780525515661 (hardback) | ISBN 9780525515692 (ebook)
Subjects: | CYAC: Best friends--Fiction. | Friendship--Fiction. | Flight--Fiction. | Snowy owl--Fiction. | Owls--Fiction.
Classification: LCC PZ7.1.B65 Maxm 2019 | DDC [E]--dc23
LC record available at https://lccn.loc.gov/2018049757
Manufactured in China by RR Donnelley Asia Printing Solutions Ltd.
ISBN 9780525515661

1 3 5 7 9 10 8 6 4 2

Edited by Jill Santopolo. Design by Ellice M. Lee. Text set in Brandon Grotesque. The art for this book was rendered in watercolor and ink on Fabriano paper, then scanned and further overworked in Photoshop by adding spot textures and colors.

MAX and **MARLA** know how to enjoy life.
It's about the simple things.

And sometimes, it's about the exciting things.

"Marla, today is a perfect day to build a kite
and let it fly high up in the sky."

They get to it right away. Max with a lot of
enthusiasm and Marla . . . well, she is helping.
A little bit. Flying is not her favorite thing,
and besides, it's rather cozy inside.

Max is adding some finishing touches.
They will make the kite extra special.
"No peeking, Marla!"

No worries. She wouldn't.

Flying is definitely not
her favorite thing.

"Here we come!"

Marla is a good friend.

"First you fly up high into the sky, and then our kite can fly right beside you. It will be almost as if we are flying together."

Marla has to think about this.

"Look, this is how it goes: You spread your wings.
You flap your wings."

"You jump!
And then . . . you fly!"

"Just don't forget to
flap your wings."

"Marla?"

Max realizes what is wrong.
"You don't have to be afraid. Owls are born to fly.
And our kite will always be flying beside you."

Marla doesn't move her wings.
Not even one flap.

"Maybe we can try again tomorrow."

Off to bed. It's been a long day,
and Marla and Max are very tired.
While the storm shakes the trees
outside, two cups of hot cocoa
and their favorite doughnuts keep
them warm and cozy.

"Whoa! Wake up, Marla! You have to see this!"

My goodness, what a mess!

The storm was not kidding. Leaves are everywhere, and their kite seems lost.

"I need your help, Marla."

"We have to clean this all up. Hey, and maybe we'll even find our kite!"

"Are you helping, Marla?"

"I can see you."

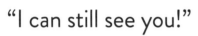
"I can still see you!"

Hmm . . . are you sure you can, Max?
Uh-oh! The wind is picking up again!

Marla gets swooped up into the clouds.

"SQUEAK!!"

she calls in utter despair.

"Marla? . . . Marla! Is that you? Let go of the kite! You were born to fly! And look, I am right there with you!"

Marla and Max are **flying together**.

Marla is a natural.

She was born to fly.

"Let's fly together again tomorrow!"

"Marla?"

"Wait for me!"

Max and Marla are best friends.